The Fairy House
Fairy Riding School

Welcome to the Fairy House —
a whole new magical world...

Look for all *The Fairy House* books

FAIRY FRIENDS
FAIRY FOR A DAY
FAIRIES TO THE RESCUE
FAIRY RIDING SCHOOL

The Fairy House
Fairy Riding School

Kelly McKain

Illustrated by Nicola Slater

■SCHOLASTIC

New York   Toronto   London   Auckland   Sydney
Mexico City   New Delhi   Hong Kong   Buenos Aires

No part of this publication may be reproduced, stored in a retrieval system, or transmitted in any form or by any means, electronic, mechanical, photocopying, recording, or otherwise, without written permission of the publisher. For information regarding permission, write to Scholastic Ltd., Euston House, 24 Eversholt Street, London NW1 1DB, United Kingdom.

Library of Congress Cataloging–in–Publication Data Available
ISBN-13: 978-0-545-04240-6
ISBN-10: 0-545-04240-2

Text copyright © 2007 by Kelly McKain
Illustrations copyright © 2007 by Nicola Slater

The rights of Kelly McKain and Nicola Slater to be identified respectively as the author and illustrator of this work have been asserted by them.

12 11 10 9 8 7 6 5 4 3 2 1   8 9 10 11 12/0

Printed in China
First Scholastic U.S.A. printing, June 2008

Chapter 1

Katie hurried out into the yard as soon as she got home from school. She ducked under the wire fence and onto the patch of rough ground beyond. The afternoon sun shone down and the almost-meadow was alive with insects buzzing around the wildflowers and with butterflies fluttering in the breeze, but Katie hardly noticed. She swished through the tall grass quickly, heading straight for the old oak tree. She had to see her new

friends, right away! She needed to ask their advice because she had a feeling she'd just done something very silly.

She reached the oak tree and spotted the dollhouse beneath it (now beautifully decorated and renamed the Fairy House). Her friends were busy enjoying the warm sunshine.

When Katie had left her pink plastic dollhouse out under the old oak tree by accident, she'd never imagined that four fairies would move in!

They'd had such wonderful times together — dancing and singing and playing fairies' games and making things and having adventures. She'd even become a fairy herself and had tried flying. And she'd rescued Daisy from the clutches of mean Tiffany, a bully in her class. It was, in fact, precisely this awful girl that Katie now needed to speak to the fairies about.

Shy little Snowdrop was watering her window boxes, her black hair tumbling forward over her pale face as she leaned out of the window. Daisy was sunbathing in a handkerchief hammock they'd hung

up between two sticks, a dreamy smile on her kind face. Fiery-red-haired Rosehip and naughty Bluebell were happily practicing gymnastics in the shorter grass under the tree, with their cute fairy skirts tucked into their underwear (and for once they weren't arguing!).

Katie giggled as Bluebell's bright blue hair stood on end as she did a handstand.

"Hi, Katie, come and play!" she called, still upside down.

Katie smiled but shook her head. "Maybe later," she said. "Right now I need your help — all of you!"

She stepped carefully over Daisy's hammock and put her little finger on the blue door handle of the Fairy House, which Bluebell had bewitched with fairy dust. "I believe in fairies, I believe in fairies, I believe in fairies," she whispered.

The top of her head tingled and there was a familiar whooshing sound in her ears as she shrank down to fairy size. Then she sat on the bench of woven grass and twigs that Bluebell had made and her fairy friends gathered around her.

"What's wrong?" asked Daisy.

"Well, you know how Tiffany made me write her story for her?" she began, and the fairies all nodded. Katie knew they were still angry about Tiffany bullying Katie into doing her homework, and worse, about her stealing the Fairy House — with poor Daisy still inside!

"Well, you know how Tiffany's father promised her a pony if she got a star for the story?"

They all nodded, and Rosehip muttered, "So unfair!"

Katie folded her arms tight. "Well, she did get a star and a pony! Now she's challenged me to be in a gymkhana this Saturday at her stables."

"What's a gymkhana?" asked Snowdrop.

"It's a competition in which you play lots of games on horses," said Rosehip, her eyes gleaming. "We had one at a summer festival in Fairyland, and I got to ride one of the Fairy Queen's ponies, remember?"

"Oh, yes!" cried Bluebell. "Do you think it will be the same for humans?"

"Probably," said Rosehip. "And it's lots of fun. You're so lucky, Katie!"

But Katie didn't feel lucky. "That's the problem," she mumbled. "I've never ridden a pony in my life. And I don't know how!"

"Oh, right. So obviously you told Tiffany no," said Rosehip. "I mean, games on horses are fun but if you don't know how to ride, you'd almost definitely fall off and hurt yourself and —"

Listening to this, Katie's face went pale. "Actually, I said yes," she told her startled friends.

"But why on earth would you do that?" Daisy asked with concern. "Like Rosehip said, it could be dangerous."

Katie took a deep breath. "While Tiffany was talking I noticed that she had a new ring on," she told them. "It had a pale green stone in it, and I'm sure it's a peridot! That's one of the birthstones we need to complete the fairy task."

The fairies' eyes all widened then. The fairy task was the reason that they were here. They needed to complete it before they would be allowed back into Fairyland.

"I made her promise that if I competed against her and won, she'd give me the ring," said Katie. "If I get

it we'll be one step closer to saving the Magic Oak."

Daisy gasped and Bluebell said, "Good thinking, Katie. Wow. You're so brave!"

Snowdrop pulled the scroll she'd been given by the Fairy Queen from her pocket and unrolled it. Once again, they all peered over her shoulder to read it. They did this every day, just to remind themselves of the importance of what they had to do. Secretly, they all hoped that some magical new instructions might appear there to make the task easier, but nothing ever did. The scroll read:

Fairy Task No. 45826

By Royal Command of the Fairy Queen

Terrible news has reached Fairyland. As you
know, the Magic Oak is the gateway between
Fairyland and the human world. The sparkling
whirlwind can only drop fairies off *here*.
Humans plan to knock down our special tree
and build a house on the land. If this happens,
fairies will no longer be able to come and help
people and the environment. You must stop
them from doing this terrible thing and make
sure that the tree is protected for the future.
Only then will you be allowed back into
Fairyland.

By order of Her Eternal Majesty

The Fairy Queen

P.S. You will need one each of the twelve
birthstones to work the magic that will save
the tree — but hurry, there's not much time!

A few days had gone by since they got the last birthstone, and the fairies were all starting to worry. Katie lay awake at night sometimes, frightened that the bulldozer was revving up that very moment, ready to come and knock down the tree. They knew that Tiffany's father, a builder, was behind the wicked plan. But until they had all the birthstones they were powerless to stop him. Without all twelve, they wouldn't be able to work the magic to save the oak tree, and Fairyland with it.

So the fairies could easily understand why Katie had decided to challenge Tiffany in order to try to win one of the birthstones. But that didn't make it any less dangerous.

"But your mom is never going to let you. Is she?" mused Snowdrop.

"She said I can go, even though neither of us like Tiffany, because she knows how much I love ponies. But she thinks I'm only having a beginner's lesson," she admitted, blushing.

"Which event do you have to beat Tiffany in?" asked Rosehip nervously.

"The Chase Me Charlie," said Katie.

"Oh. I haven't heard of that," Rosehip said.

"I'm sure it's easy-breezy," said Bluebell helpfully, but Katie didn't feel any better.

"Maybe you could look it up in a book?" Daisy suggested.

"Good idea," said Katie. "I'll look in the school library tomorrow. It's too bad I can't learn how to ride from

a book, too! What on earth am I going to do?"

"Maybe we can help," said Rosehip suddenly. "You remember when you took the Fairy House inside and we got a little bit, well . . ."

"Naughty, and wrecked every-thing," finished Bluebell.

"Well, we brought your toy ponies to life with fairy dust, didn't we?" Rosehip continued, thoughtfully. "I was just thinking that if we brought them out here and, well, there's not much time, but maybe —"

Katie leaped to her feet, suddenly under-standing her. "We could bring them to life and you could teach me to ride!" she cried.

"Wow, Rosehip, what a great idea!" gasped Snowdrop.

"Well, don't get too excited, there's hardly any time and —" Rosehip was saying. But Katie didn't hear her, she'd already grabbed the enchanted door handle and was busy turning big. "I'll be right back!" she called, as she rushed inside to get her toy ponies.

For the first time since she'd agreed to the gymkhana, Katie felt a rush of excitement about it. Rosehip's riding lessons would give her a chance against Tiffany. Only a teeny tiny chance, of course, but a chance all the same.

Katie knew she had to try.

After all, they really needed that birthstone.

Chapter 2

A few minutes later, Katie was back at the Fairy House with the toy ponies, a bottle of water that her mom had insisted she bring out to drink, and a blue cotton bag bulging with something mysterious. She had also changed out of her school uniform and into jeans and a T-shirt.

"Good idea, Katie," said Rosehip, nodding toward her clothes. "Much better for riding."

"What's in the bag?" asked Bluebell,

who couldn't bear not knowing everything, right away.

Katie smiled, knelt down carefully,
and tipped the contents of the bag out
onto the grass. The fairies gasped at
the array of pony care equipment in
front of them. There were grooming
brushes and combs and ribbons and
elastics. It all looked great, except . . .

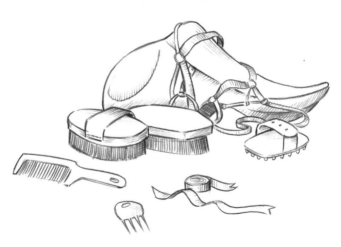

"Oh, no, there's only one bridle and
saddle set," Snowdrop cried.

The fairies' wings all drooped with disappointment.

"We were hoping we could all learn together," said Daisy sadly.

But Bluebell didn't give up that easily. After a moment she picked up the bridle and studied it, then said, "Don't worry, I can make these from daisies and we can ride bareback!"

"How clever, Bluebell!" Snowdrop said, and they all cheered up again.

Katie stood the five plastic ponies (well, four ponies and one unicorn!) up on a flat place in the grass. Once she took hold of the enchanted door handle and turned small again, it was time to get down to business.

While Daisy helped Bluebell gather daisies for the bridles, Rosehip and Snowdrop made a ring of twigs and woven grass for the ponies to ride in.

"If we're bewitching them with fairy dust to come alive, they're going to need water, just like real ponies," said Rosehip. "I wonder how . . ."

But Katie had a good idea about that. She and Snowdrop went into the Fairy House and up to the bathroom. Together they dragged the tub down the stairs (fairies don't take baths and they'd thought the tub was for mixing potions or playing hide-and-seek in!). They set it up beside the ring and, with Daisy's help, they carefully tipped over Katie's water bottle and filled the tub right to the top, making the perfect pony drinking trough.

Then Daisy had the idea to make safety helmets from the unripe nuts of the buckeye tree near the edge of the almost-meadow. Bluebell flew up to get them, then stamped on the green shells to open them up (she was very good at stamping!).

Soon everything was ready, and it was time to enchant the ponies — Katie and the fairies were so excited they couldn't help dancing around and squealing with joy! Snowdrop took the tiny bottle of fairy dust from her pocket and walked nervously up to the white unicorn that she'd ridden when the fairies were being naughty in Katie's house. She stroked his mane and gave him a longing look.

"That one can be yours," Katie told her, smiling. "His name is Moondust."

Snowdrop beamed at Katie, then shook a little of the fairy dust into her palm and rubbed it onto the end of the unicorn's nose. From

mane to tail, he rippled with a sheen of sparkles, and then suddenly he was a real, live unicorn. He whinnied with glee and nuzzled up to Snowdrop, looking very happy to see her again.

For herself, Katie chose the pretty pink pony called Rainbow. He had a multicolored mane and tail. She could hardly believe that only yesterday she'd been playing with him in her bedroom — she never imagined that

she would get to ride him for real! When she rubbed the fairy dust onto his nose he came shimmering to life, then whinnied and trotted happily around the ring.

Next, Bluebell chose the blue pony with the purple mane and tail, which Katie said was named Damson. Daisy took the yellow one, Sunshine, with her pure-white mane and tail, and Rosehip got Poppy, a beautiful orange pony who licked her hand almost as soon as she rubbed the fairy dust onto her nose.

Then Katie heaved the saddle off the twig fence and strode bravely toward Rainbow. "We have to get started right away," she told Rosehip anxiously. "My mom will be calling me in for dinner soon and there's so much to learn."

But Rosehip just smiled at her. "You need to get to know your pony first and make friends," she said. "So put that saddle back and grab a grooming brush."

Katie felt very lucky that she had a friend who could really show her the ropes, and soon they were all busy grooming their ponies. Daisy parted Sunshine's tail into two braids with daisy ties just like hers, and Snowdrop combed out Moondust's mane until it was sleek and shiny. Bluebell brushed out Damson's purple mane and tail to match her own hair, and Rosehip styled Poppy's into cascading waves. As for Katie, she wove some pink ribbons into Rainbow's tail and then tied her own hair up with the rest.

Then Rosehip said it was time to ride, and Katie felt a flutter of nerves and excitement in her chest as she

hurried back to the fence to get the saddle and bridle.

Rosehip helped them all put their bridles on, and showed Katie how to do up the buckles under the saddle. Then, with their buckeye-shell helmets safely strapped on, they mounted up, ready to start their very first riding lesson.

They began by walking around the edge of the ring, with Rosehip leading the way on Poppy, calling out instructions. After a while, Katie got the hang of turning Rainbow at the corners so that they didn't keep getting stuck at the fence. Everyone was doing very well, except Bluebell. She

loved the riding, but she didn't like being told what to do by Rosehip. Not one little bit.

"Why can't *I* be the teacher?" she whined.

Rosehip wheeled Poppy around and trotted expertly up to Bluebell. "Because it was my idea and because I'm the only one who has ever ridden before!" she said.

"That still doesn't mean you know *everything*!" Bluebell grumbled.

"Bluebell, just stop complaining, sit up straight, and shorten your reins," ordered Rosehip, which seemed to annoy Bluebell even more!

Katie was far too excited to complain about anything. She was getting to ride a pony for the very first time, and it felt amazing. She'd always wanted to try riding, but her mom never had the money to pay for lessons.

Katie beamed — riding was just so much fun, especially when Rosehip showed them how to trot. Katie seemed to bump around a lot more than the fairies, who naturally moved with the ponies' rhythms, so Rosehip showed her how to use her stirrups to stand up and down. It took a while to get it right, but once she did, she just couldn't stop grinning — she was starting to feel like a real rider.

Poor Snowdrop wasn't having such an easy time, though. Moondust only wanted to go galloping off so she had to keep pulling the reins to slow him down. And Daisy was having the opposite problem, as Sunshine would hardly go anywhere! Instead, she kept dropping back to walk and wandering over to the edge of the ring to munch at the grass.

"Come on, Daisy, you're supposed to be in charge of that pony!" shouted Rosehip, but Daisy didn't seem too worried — she was just as dreamy as Sunshine!

Katie was having so much fun that she almost didn't hear her mom calling her in for dinner. Reluctantly, she leaped off Rainbow and gave him a big pat for being so good. Then she raced back over to the Fairy House, grabbed the enchanted door handle and tingled and whooshed herself big again. She called good-bye to her friends as she hurried away, promising them that she'd come back right after school the next afternoon — hopefully with a book that explained what the Chase Me Charlie was.

Katie walked through the kitchen door with a heart full of joy and a head full of ponies, ponies, ponies!

Thanks to her wonderful friends, she might *not* actually fall off in the competition!

And maybe, just maybe, she would have a teensy-weensy chance of beating Tiffany.

Chapter 3

The next afternoon, Katie arrived at the Fairy House with a library book clutched in her hand. She put the book down on the grass and then turned small as her friends hurried out to greet her.

"I found this book! It says in the index that the Chase Me Charlie is explained on page thirty-five," she told them with a grin.

Together they flipped through the pages, which were as tall as them.

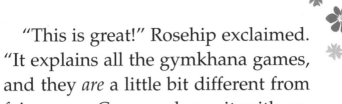

"This is great!" Rosehip exclaimed. "It explains all the gymkhana games, and they *are* a little bit different from fairy ones. Can you leave it with us, Katie, so I can read up on what to teach you?"

"Of course," said Katie. She thought again about how lucky she was to have Rosehip for a riding instructor.

When they reached page thirty-five, they all nervously knelt over the book.

"In the Chase Me Charlie, the competitors jump over higher and higher poles," Rosehip read aloud. "If you knock a pole down you're out. The last person left in is the winner."

Katie stared at her, shocked. "But Rosehip," she cried. "I hardly know how to ride *at all*, let alone *jump*! What am I going to do?"

She looked so panicked that Bluebell and Snowdrop quickly closed the book, so Katie wouldn't keep staring at the photograph of a girl and pony leaping over an enormous red-and-white-striped pole. Daisy put her arm around Katie's trembling shoulders and said gently, "Don't worry, you don't have to do it. It sounds far too dangerous. Just tell Tiffany that you won't do it and we'll find another way of getting the birthstone."

Katie really wanted to back out, but she shook her head. She couldn't let the fairies down. "Thanks, but I promised I'd help you in any way I could, and that's what I'm going to do," she told them. "This could be our only chance to get that stone. I've got to go for it."

"Good for you, Katie," cried Bluebell. "We know you can do it!"

"And look how quickly you learned to trot. I'm sure you'll be jumping in no time!" said Rosehip encouragingly.

Then the fairies all hugged Katie, and told her how brave she was. She wasn't so sure about that, but she had to learn to ride, and she was determined to do her best. She forced the dreaded Chase Me Charlie to the back of her mind, and concentrated

on trotting Rainbow around the ring behind Snowdrop and Moondust.

"Why can't we canter yet?" Bluebell called out to Rosehip, swinging her legs back and forth impatiently.

"Let's just spend a little bit more time trotting first," Rosehip said firmly.

But Bluebell didn't want to spend a little bit more time trotting first — Bluebell wanted to canter! And nothing Rosehip said was going to stop her.

She gave Damson a hefty kick in the sides and the pony flew forward into a canter, past the others, heading right for the fence. Bluebell shrieked in fright and shouted, "Abandon pony!" leaping off just as he jumped. She shot into the air, turning somersaults, flapping her wings desperately, but she just couldn't

get control. She tumbled downward and landed with a splash in the water trough!

The fairies and Katie gasped, but when Bluebell emerged, blowing out a big mouthful of water like a fish in a fountain, they all burst into fits of laughter.

After some more trotting, Rosehip said, "Bluebell has kindly demonstrated the *wrong* way to go into a canter. Now I will show you the *right* way," and she and Poppy romped around the ring in perfect rhythm.

When Katie tried, she thought it was the most amazing feeling she'd ever had in her life — easily as good as becoming a fairy and flying.

After several more canters, it was time to head home. Katie had had so much fun she couldn't help grinning to herself all through dinner. When Katie's mom asked what she'd been doing, she replied, "Oh, nothing much, just playing with my toy ponies in the almost-meadow. I made a riding ring and pretended to have a lesson and learned how to canter and everything!"

Katie's mom beamed. "That's great, darling. And when you go to the stables on Saturday you'll get to ride a pony for real!"

"I bet it will be wonderful," said Katie, still smiling to herself. She couldn't tell her mom that she'd just

been riding a pony. Like most adults, her mom couldn't see fairies — and so she was unlikely to believe that Katie was being taught to ride an enchanted pony by one.

She just hoped that Rosehip really could get her jumping by Saturday.

When Katie came swishing through the tall grass of the almost-meadow the following afternoon, her friends were already busy in the paddock, and they waved and called out greetings as she approached. Her stomach flipped with excitement as she paused by the Fairy House to turn small and then hurried over to them.

"Oh, wow!" she cried, dashing up to Daisy, who was busy painting a stick with blue and red stripes. "They look just like the jumping poles in my book!"

"Yes, we've been busy all day building things for the gymkhana games!" said Bluebell proudly.

Katie saw that they'd brought the plastic chairs out of the kitchen, and Rosehip and Snowdrop were busy painting them with matching stripes.

Just then, Rainbow trotted up and Katie made a big fuss over him, patting him and ruffling his mane. The other ponies were happily milling around the paddock, chomping on grass and drinking from the water trough that Bluebell had fallen in.

Grinning, Katie grabbed a brush and started helping Daisy paint the jumping poles.

Soon everything was ready, so Katie and the fairies gave their ponies a good brushing and put their bridles on. Then it was time to ride!

As they mounted, Katie felt nerves and excitement building in her chest.

"Let's start with the Chase Me Charlie," said Rosehip as they walked their ponies around the ring, warming up. "After all, that's the game you need to beat Tiffany at to get the birthstone, so that's the one that matters most."

Katie gulped — the Chase Me Charlie was also the scariest game

by far, because she'd have to jump. But she was determined to try her best — she really didn't want to let her friends down.

Rosehip sprang expertly off Poppy and set up the jump. She balanced a striped pole on the lowest rung of two chair backs and put another on the ground below, as a guide for the ponies.

Then they all lined up to try jumping it.

Rosehip went first, to show them how it was done. She and Poppy leaped effortlessly over the pole and landed at a canter on the other side. Bluebell volunteered to go next. She raced up to the pole and made a good jump, but on the way down the pole wobbled a lot! It stayed on, though, which meant she was still in the game.

Then Snowdrop and Moondust tried — and Moondust leaped so high over the pole that Snowdrop had to cling on for dear life!

"I forgot to mention that unicorns are excellent jumpers!" called Rosehip, as Snowdrop caught her breath.

"If only I could ride *Moondust* in the gymkhana, I'd beat Tiffany easily!" said Katie with a sigh, making them all giggle.

"Can you imagine her face if you rode out on a unicorn?" chuckled Bluebell.

It was fun to imagine — but of course the birthstone had to be won fair and square. Turning Moondust big and riding him in the gymkhana wouldn't be fair at all!

Next, Daisy and Sunshine trotted

lazily over the pole and it fell loudly to the ground.

"You're out because you knocked the pole down," Rosehip told Daisy, but Daisy just smiled and let Sunshine's reins slide through her hands so that the pony could eat the grass. Neither of them seemed to care about jumping higher, anyway!

Katie took a deep breath. There was no more putting it off. Everyone else had jumped, and it was definitely her turn. She gathered all her courage and cantered toward the jump. But at the last minute she lost her nerve and pulled on her reins so that Rainbow swerved away.

Rosehip was very nice and said she could try again, but Katie just made Rainbow swerve out again. Her hands were shaking and her heart

was thumping in her chest. "I've got to jump!" she wailed. "But I'm just too frightened! Oh, what am I going to do?"

"Why don't we try some of the other games," Rosehip suggested. "Getting upset about the jumping will just make it harder."

Katie agreed, feeling relieved.

The gymkhana games turned out to be a lot of fun. They played musical chairs, with Rosehip singing fairy songs as they rode around in a circle. When she stopped singing they all had to leap off their ponies and dash to sit down. They were having so much fun that Bluebell didn't even complain when she was the first one out, and she happily helped Rosehip with the singing instead.

Then they set out two lines of three

chairs and took turns weaving around them to the far end of the ring and back again, just like it showed in the book. Katie and Bluebell were neck and neck as the first pair, but with Moondust galloping at top speed, Snowdrop went ahead at the end.

Then they did the flag race, and Daisy said she'd be the judge so Rosehip could have a chance to ride. Katie raced Snowdrop to the end of the paddock to grab one colored flag each and when they got back  they tagged Rosehip and Bluebell, who both set off at a furious gallop! They played this game again and again just for the fun of it, and soon

Katie was really enjoying zooming across the ring and whizzing around the tight turn at the end.

When they finally paused to catch their breath, Katie remembered the more serious matter at hand — beating Tiffany. But there was no time to try the Chase Me Charlie again — she'd promised her mom she'd be in after an hour, because they were going to visit Aunt Jane.

On Friday afternoon there was no avoiding the jump — the gymkhana was the very next day, and it was Katie's last chance to try the Chase Me Charlie. As soon as she got to the almost-meadow and turned small, she hurried right to the paddock. Her friends were already mounted and trotting around on their ponies, warming up. She called to them, "This

is my last chance to practice, so I'd better try the Chase Me Charlie one more time." Then she strode over to Rainbow to get him saddled up.

Katie tried the Chase Me Charlie again and again, but she was still too scared to jump, and every time she failed, she just got more and more upset with herself. Then when she finally *did* force herself to jump, with her eyes tight shut and squealing in fright, Rainbow got confused and knocked the pole with his back hoof. Rosehip told her it was great that she jumped at all. She wanted Katie to try again, but suddenly Katie's mom was calling her in for dinner and their time was up.

Katie dismounted and sadly gave Rainbow a big pat. After all, he'd done a great job. It wasn't his fault she was a scaredy-cat!

"Can't you just use magic so I can win?" Katie asked her friends desperately, trying one more time to find a way out of doing the gymkhana.

The fairies shook their heads. "That's too big a spell for us," said Daisy sadly.

Katie glanced hopefully at Rosehip. "Or . . . maybe, you could turn big and do it *for* me, like when Bluebell took my place at school," she suggested.

But the little fairy just gave her a hug and said, "Sorry, Katie, but Tiffany challenged *you*, so you have to do it yourself. Otherwise, even if we win, you won't be able to get the peridot ring."

Katie sighed. There was no way around it. She *had* to ride against Tiffany. She hugged her friends good-bye, turned big again, and with a

heavy heart trudged back toward the garden fence.

After dinner she told her mom she was extra tired and went upstairs early, still feeling upset. As she lay in bed, she wondered how on earth she was even going to get over the first jump in the Chase Me Charlie, let alone actually win it!

Chapter 4

The next morning, Tiffany's nanny, Lisa, picked Katie up and she sat alone in the backseat of the car — Tiffany had insisted on sitting in the front, of course, which was fine with Katie.

As she gazed out of the open window, her stomach churned with nerves and excitement about the gymkhana. Then suddenly she gasped — the four fairies were zooming alongside the car, waving at her!

She put her hand out of the window and they grabbed on as she pulled them in. They fell into her lap in a panting, messy heap — they were not used to flying so fast!

"Surprise!" cried Bluebell. "We're coming to watch!"

Katie beamed in delight — with her friends there to support her, things would be much more fun.

"And you'll need some real riding clothes for the gymkhana," Rosehip said. "You can't go in those scruffy jeans and old school shoes."

The fairies exchanged mischievous looks and, with a sprinkling of fairy dust, Katie's clothes shimmered and changed into fabulous riding gear, all pink and purple. She had a real safety helmet and shiny black riding boots and everything. As Katie gazed down at herself in disbelief, Daisy whispered,

"Katie-ella, you shall go to the gymkhana!"

They all giggled at that and as Katie joined in, Tiffany turned around quickly in her seat. The fairies ducked down out of sight. Her eyes widened when she saw Katie in her colorful new clothes. "How did you do that?" she demanded. "What happened to your scruffy jeans?"

Katie shrugged. "I got changed. I had my riding things in my bag. It's amazing what you can find at the town flea market if you look hard enough," she added quickly, in

case Tiffany tried to ask where she got the outfit.

"You might look good, but you'll never beat me in the Chase Me Charlie," said Tiffany. Then she turned back around and sulked.

The words "Chase Me Charlie" made Katie panic. "I can't go," she hissed as the fairies flew up from near her feet. "I can't do it."

"You'll be OK," said Daisy gently. "Just do your best."

"But make sure you win, OK?" Bluebell added cheerfully. "After all, the future of your world *and* Fairyland depends on it!"

"Bluebell, just be quiet!" cried Snowdrop, but Katie knew she was right. They needed to collect all twelve birthstones to save the tree and this was a chance to get one. This was no time to panic.

They turned into the stables and the car stopped. Tiffany jumped out and marched up the path, not even waiting for Katie. Heart pounding, Katie climbed out, too, and thanked Lisa for the ride. Then she walked quickly toward the office, with the fairies flying high above her so they wouldn't be spotted. She was about to walk in when she noticed Tiffany standing by the desk, so she hid around the corner and peeked inside. The fairies fluttered silently through the door, though, and landed on a beam high above Tiffany's head.

"There," Katie heard Tiffany say to herself as she wrote something on a list. "Let's see how perfect little Katie does with Ebony. If she can even get on, that is! He's so fierce she'll probably be thrown off before she's even in

the ring. There's no way she's getting my peridot ring!"

And with a nasty laugh she marched out of the door.

Katie pressed herself behind it, breathing hard. What a sneak! Tiffany had signed her up to ride an impossible pony! She should have guessed she'd do something like this, just to make absolutely sure Katie wouldn't win.

Katie felt utterly terrified and the last bit of confidence she'd built up with her fairy friends in the almost-meadow slipped away. As they flew out of the office to meet her, she looked into their faces, hoping to see encouraging smiles, but they looked just as worried as she did.

Katie gulped. She knew that was a bad sign.

A very bad sign indeed.

The fairies and Katie spent the next few minutes peeking over the stable door at Ebony — and trembling.

Finally, Katie found the courage to open the door, but she'd only taken one step inside when the pony began snorting and pawing the ground,

teeth gnashing. Terrified, she squealed and ran back out again, right into a very smug-looking Tiffany. "Are you enjoying your pony?" she asked with a smirk.

"How could you do this to me?" Katie cried. "There's no way I can ride *him*!"

Tiffany just grinned and said, "Looks like you'll have to drop out of the gymkhana, doesn't it?"

Just then, Katie caught a glimpse of her friends doing something that appeared to involve fairy dust and silent chanting above Tiffany's head. As soon as Tiffany left, she demanded to know what they'd been up to.

"Oh, nothing!" Bluebell giggled. "We've just put a fairy spell on her, that's all."

Katie narrowed her eyes at them, worried. "What fairy spell?" she asked,

but the fairies just smiled and looked very naughty.

"Oh, don't worry!" said Daisy. "Just a little something to make sure that if you do win, she plays fair and gives you the ring."

"Now, let's get started grooming your pony," said Rosehip. "We don't have much time."

Katie stared at her. "Are you crazy?" she cried. "There's no way I'm going in that stable!"

Rosehip nodded. "I understand. Don't worry, I'll go in first and have a little word with Ebony."

Katie was completely confused by this. "A little word?" she repeated. "How can you have a little word with a *pony*?"

Rosehip just grinned at her and flew into the stable — only the slight tremble in her wings gave away the

fact that she was nervous, too. The other fairies perched on the stable door to watch and Katie peered in, from a safe distance.

Rosehip fluttered slowly up to Ebony and landed on his water bucket. Katie started to worry that he might simply knock her in and drink her up, but instead he just lowered his great black head and snorted at her.

"Rosehip, be careful!" Katie whispered in alarm as she watched her friend climb up the pony's velvety mane and lie flat along it, so that her head was up by his ear.

Then she began to whisper to him so quietly that Katie couldn't even

hear what she was saying. She paused once in a while to listen to his snorts.

"Ebony says that the owner of the stables is trying to sell him because he keeps bucking and rearing and dumping riders on the ground," Rosehip said softly.

Katie stiffened, frightened. She didn't like the sound of being dumped on the ground at all!

"But no one will buy him because he's so bad-tempered," Rosehip continued, stroking the pony's ear.

As Rosehip whispered and listened some more, Ebony's snorts became gentler and gentler until they were just soft whinnies. His whole body seemed to relax and Katie was sure that even though no fairy dust was involved, she was still watching a very special kind of magic.

"He's saying that he's only naughty because he's lonely and bored," Rosehip told them.

Katie felt a little sorry for Ebony when she heard that. Even though he scared her, she certainly knew what it was like to feel lonely and bored. Before she'd met her fairy friends, she'd had to fill long hours playing by herself.

"Poor Ebony!" sighed Snowdrop.

"Never mind poor Ebony!" Katie cried in panic. "What about poor *me*? He just told you he likes to dump riders on the ground!"

But Rosehip just giggled. "Don't worry," she said, "he's promised to be good for you this afternoon.

"And he says that all he wants is to get out of this yard where nobody likes him, and find one special little girl to love," Rosehip added.

"Aw!" said the other fairies.

In no time, Ebony was far more relaxed. Rosehip gave his ears a final stroke and then flew back to the stable door as he began happily munching on his hay.

Katie stared in at Ebony. She still didn't completely trust him, but she would have to try. Barely able to breathe, she opened the stable door and stepped inside. But this time Ebony just nuzzled her hand in greeting, and allowed her to lead him out of the stable and tie him up in the yard.

Soon she was carefully grooming him until his black coat shone, and

putting ribbons in his mane and tail, just as she'd practiced on Rainbow. When she finished, he looked like the handsomest pony in the whole world. Rosehip gave her a hand tacking up, and soon she found herself swinging into Ebony's saddle and heading toward the main yard.

As she rode to her place at the far side of the ring, Katie tried to swallow her nerves and be a good sport, saying, "Good luck," to the other riders as she passed them. They all smiled and wished her luck, too, except Tiffany, of course. At first she looked shocked to see Katie riding at all, then she sneered, "You may have managed to get on that pony, but you'll never *stay* on!"

But Katie didn't reply. The whistle had blown and it was time for the gymkhana to begin.

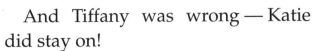

And Tiffany was wrong — Katie did stay on!

They played games similar to the ones that she'd practiced with the fairies in the almost-meadow, and Ebony was a dream, doing exactly what he was asked and really trying his best. She soon forgot all her worries and started enjoying herself, especially when she caught sight of the fairies, sitting on the fence near her, and cheering her on, each hidden behind a piece of riding gear!

Katie was really cheered up by the look of surprise on Tiffany's face as she and Ebony won third place in the obstacle course (round cones, not chairs this time, but the idea was the same). And Tiffany's surprise soon turned to annoyance when Katie and Ebony tied for second in the flag race with a girl named Ingrid.

When the first round of games was over, everyone dismounted and had a drink of water. Tiffany said to Katie, "I don't know how you made that pony behave but believe me, it won't last. He'll be back to his old tricks in the Chase Me Charlie, and then you'll be on the ground! Just you wait!"

Katie tried to ignore Tiffany's unkind words, but she couldn't help getting a little upset. Her stomach twisted with nerves as she watched the jump being set up. But even if Ebony did behave (and she really hoped Rosehip was right and Tiffany was wrong about that!) she had no idea if she'd clear the first jump . . . or if she'd be brave enough to try at all.

Chapter 5

Katie took a deep breath and tried to stop her hands from trembling on the reins. It was time for the Chase Me Charlie. There were three other girls competing in her age group — Tiffany, of course, and Sophie and Becky, who introduced themselves as they all waited for the jumps to be set up. They both said they'd done lots of jumping before, which made Katie even more nervous.

Then the judge signaled that the competition was starting and they all lined up for the first round.

The first pole was very low and the others all effortlessly jumped clear. Then it was Katie's turn. She closed her eyes and squealed as Ebony trotted over the pole — he hardly seemed to notice that it was there. It wasn't a great performance, but the pole stayed up and she was still in the game.

As she trotted Ebony past the fairies on the fence, they all gave her a big cheer and she managed to give them a little smile. Her heart was thumping hard — she'd gotten over the first jump. Now she just had to keep going.

In the next round, Sophie misjudged the distance and knocked the pole down, which shocked everyone.

But Katie managed to get over it again, and this time it was with her eyes open, so she was able to steer a little better!

Then, with three of them still in, the pole was moved up again.

As she waited her turn, Katie reached down to give Ebony a big pat and he snorted happily — he was

being absolutely wonderful. There were no traces of his nastiness left at all, and he seemed to be enjoying the competition enormously.

However, one person who wasn't pleased with his performance was Tiffany, and as Katie neared the third pole, she shouted, "Stop, there's a bee on you!" really loudly.

For a fleeting moment, Katie panicked, but then she realized that there was no bee and that Tiffany was just trying to trick her. That only made her more determined to succeed and she jumped clear!

But so had Becky and Tiffany, and the pole went up again. Katie ruffled her pony's mane and said to him, "Come on, Ebony, let's show them what we're made of!"

This time, she cantered at the jump and cleared it easily. Her stomach

flipped with excitement and she couldn't help smiling. They were doing it — they were actually doing it! The only problem was that Tiffany and Becky cleared it, too, so they had to keep going.

Once again in the next round, the pole went up and this time the height made Katie gulp, especially when Becky knocked it down and was out.

Only she and Tiffany remained, going head-to-head for first place.

Tiffany gave Katie a nasty look, then pushed her pony into a canter and flew awkwardly over the jump — for a moment the pole wobbled and Katie thought it was going to come off. But no such luck! She had to jump again. The pole had gotten really high and she wasn't sure whether they'd make it.

Katie cantered around the corner and lined herself up with the pole. She was so busy thinking about how high it was that she looked at the ground as they jumped instead of looking forward. As Ebony lifted off, Katie started to fall! She made herself focus and held on tight and managed to get her balance back. The pole stayed on and so did she! But Katie and Ebony only made it over by the skin of their teeth, and Katie felt nervous. She was sure they'd be out in the next round.

Bluebell whistled and Katie looked toward

the fence as she rode back to the starting line. The fairies had all picked dandelions, which they were now using as pom-poms, singing, "Katie, Katie, ra-ra-ra, Katie is a superstar!"

That certainly made her smile! She felt her confidence coming back, knowing how much her friends believed in her.

As Tiffany turned toward the fence she said to Katie, "I'm going to win, so you may as well give up now. I'll just keep jumping higher and higher until you and that useless nag lose!"

Katie leaned over to hug Ebony's neck — he wasn't a useless nag, he was a fabulous star pony! When Katie looked up again, Tiffany was heading for the jump. But she made a clumsy approach and as they took off, her pony's back foot knocked the pole. It wibbled and wobbled and then — *thunk!* — it was on the ground.

Katie stared at the pole. She couldn't believe it. Tiffany was out! All she had to do to win was jump this final pole!

As she gathered her reins, Katie caught sight of the fairies peeking out from behind their dandelions, hardly

able to watch. Katie tried to ignore Tiffany's whining as she blamed her pony for the bad jump. She needed a clear head to do this. She circled Ebony around and asked him to trot early, giving herself plenty of time. Then when she was heading right for the jump she sped Ebony up to a canter and urged him on with her heels. "Come on, Eb!" she called. "We can do this, I know we can!"

They neared the jump and she gritted her teeth and bobbed forward. Ebony jumped into the air, over the pole, and . . . they won!

Katie gave a shout of joy, and Ebony whinnied and cantered her past the fairies so quickly that she couldn't even turn her head to see them. She heard their cheers, though, and Bluebell singing the ra-ra-ra song.

Everyone in the small crowd was clapping as Katie slowed Ebony to a trot, then a walk. She caught sight of a girl about the same age as her, with short dark hair, clapping especially hard. Ebony was watching her, too, and Katie wondered who she was.

Then she noticed the judge coming toward her, so she dismounted, shook hands with him, and took her blue ribbon, which she tied proudly onto Ebony's bridle. When Tiffany was handed the second-place ribbon, she didn't even say thank you. The judge was still standing there

beside them and Katie realized they were supposed to shake hands. She offered hers to Tiffany, who reluctantly took it.

"Well done," mumbled Tiffany, looking away.

"Thanks," said Katie brightly. "You, too."

"I can't believe you did that!" Tiffany added. "I thought you'd never ridden before."

Katie just grinned. "Beginner's luck, I guess," she said with a twinkle in her eye.

Then she turned and led Ebony out of the ring and back to his stable, almost skipping with sheer delight, the fairies flying high above her. Once they were safely out of sight, the fairies zoomed down and grabbed Katie in hugs, yelling their congratulations.

"Thank you all for helping me," said Katie. "Especially you, Rosehip."

"It was nothing," said Rosehip, but she was glowing with pride.

After they all made a huge fuss over Ebony, too, Katie went to find Tiffany to claim her real prize — the peridot ring!

She found Tiffany by her pony's stall, sulkily grooming him while scolding him for not winning.

"I've come for the ring," Katie said.

"What?" Tiffany replied, without looking up. "I don't know what you're talking about."

Katie felt queasy. She'd won fair and square — surely Tiffany would have to give it to her. "You promised to give me your ring if I beat you," she said weakly.

"Sorry, I don't remember," said Tiffany shortly.

Just then, Katie felt a fairy land on her ponytail. "Don't worry," a voice whispered in her ear. Katie could tell that it was Bluebell. "This is why we worked the fairy magic on her earlier — we had a feeling she might try to back out of her promise."

Just then, Tiffany shrieked and jumped backward. She held her hand up in the air and stared at it in horror. Katie gasped when she saw Tiffany's finger. It was the one on which she wore the peridot ring. It had turned bright green and had swollen up to the size of a plum.

Katie hid her smile. "Give me the ring," she demanded.

"No!" cried Tiffany, and her finger swelled up to the size of an apple. She

stared at Katie. "H-h-how are you doing this?" she cried.

Katie looked her steadily in the eye. "Give me the ring," she repeated.

"No!" yelled Tiffany, and with that, her finger swelled up to the size of a melon. Alarmed, Tiffany cried, "All right, you can have it!" and she tried to tug the ring off. As soon as she touched it, her finger returned to its normal size and color and the ring slid off. Katie could hear giggling in the air around her, and Rosehip whispered in her ear, "Quick, get it before she changes her mind."

Katie held out her hand and Tiffany dropped the ring into her palm. She was still staring at her finger, wondering if what she'd just seen was real or not. "How did you —" she began, but Katie and the fairies were gone, hurrying back to Ebony.

Once they were safely around the corner the fairies landed on the stable door and burst into giggles. Bluebell laughed so much she almost fell off! "That was very naughty," said Katie, but she couldn't help smiling, too.

Suddenly, they heard footsteps coming toward them. The fairies all flew backward into the stable, thinking it was Tiffany.

But instead, it was the girl with the short dark hair. The one who'd clapped so hard when Katie and Ebony had won the Chase Me Charlie. Relieved, Katie gave her a big smile.

"I'm Lily Rose," said the girl shyly. "I've come to see Ebony."

Chapter 6

Lily Rose gave Ebony a huge hug, burying her face in his mane, and he nuzzled into her affectionately. "Oh, I just love this pony so much," she sighed.

"Me, too," said Katie.

Lily Rose straightened up, looking nervous. "You're not buying him, are you?" she asked.

"Oh, no!" cried Katie. "But, is that what *you* want to do?"

Lily Rose hugged Ebony tight again and nodded. She told Katie that she'd come to the stables with her father, looking for a pony to buy. "I fell in love with Ebony right away," she explained. "But the owner told us he was bad-tempered and dangerous, so Dad wouldn't even let me try riding him."

"He was just lonely and bored," Katie explained. "He'll be fine now. All he wants is someone to love who'll love him back. You're the perfect person."

Lily Rose beamed. "Yes, I am," she said.

Katie caught sight of the hovering fairies. They all had huge grins on their faces.

"I've just got to persuade my dad that Ebony really is safe," said Lily Rose. "He was impressed with the way he behaved for you, but he wants to see me ride him myself."

In a flash, Katie loaned Lily Rose her riding hat and boosted her into the saddle. Then she and the fairies hurried to the side of the ring to watch, with all their fingers crossed for luck.

Lily Rose rode Ebony perfectly and when her father said that she could buy him Ebony whinnied with delight — he seemed to understand that he'd found a special friend, without Rosehip even having to translate!

That's when Katie glanced into the parking lot and saw Tiffany's car driving away. "Oh, stop! Wait!" she cried,

running after it, but the car was soon out of sight. Katie walked back into the yard, shoulders drooping, trying not to cry. She couldn't believe Tiffany was mean enough to leave her behind. How on earth was she going to get home now?

Luckily, Lily Rose asked her what was wrong, and Katie explained what Tiffany had done. "That's no problem, we'll take you home," Lily Rose's dad said kindly.

So when he'd spoken to the owner about Ebony, and Katie had called her mom from the office to make sure it was OK to get a ride with someone else, they set off — but not before the fairies quickly changed Katie's riding outfit back into her normal clothes. Katie didn't want her mom asking too many questions! Tired out from all the pom-pom waving, the fairies

hitched a ride with Ebony in the horse trailer.

When they all arrived at Katie's house, her mom came out to greet them. Katie introduced her to Lily Rose and her dad, and Ebony, of course. "I even got to ride on him and got this," she told her, holding up her blue ribbon for her mom to see.

Lily Rose laughed. "Oh, Katie, don't be silly!" she cried. "It was more than —" She stopped suddenly as Katie gave her a quick shake of her head — she didn't want her mom to know she'd been cantering and jumping in the gymkhana — that would be very difficult to explain!

Before Lily Rose got back in the car, she gave Katie a big hug and invited her to come over anytime. "I'd love to

see you again," she said, "and so would Ebony."

"Thanks. You, too," said Katie happily.

As they stood waving good-bye, only Katie saw the fairies come whizzing out of the horse trailer and zoom high up into the air above them. Her mom beamed and pulled her close. "I'm so glad you had fun, darling," she said, "and how wonderful that you made such a nice new friend! I wish you could go

riding every week, but it's just so expensive."

Katie smiled up at her mom and said, "Don't worry, I'm sure I'll get the chance to ride again soon."

She heard giggling at this and glanced around to find the four fairies swimming in the birdbath. She couldn't help grinning, too, knowing that she could ride the enchanted ponies in the almost-meadow whenever she liked.

As her mom went indoors to make dinner, Katie hurried over to her friends. She took the peridot ring from her pocket and they all watched it sparkle in the sunshine.

"That's four birthstones we've got," she said proudly. "Maybe we really *can* save the oak tree!"

"Hip-hip-hooray for Katie!" cried

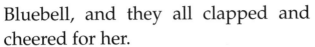

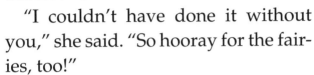

Bluebell, and they all clapped and cheered for her.

"I couldn't have done it without you," she said. "So hooray for the fairies, too!"

"Hip-hip-hooray for the fairies!" they all cried gleefully, splashing around in the birdbath. Then they all said good-bye and Katie waved to them as they fluttered off high into the air, back to the almost-meadow and the Fairy House.

And as she wandered indoors, Katie couldn't help wondering what kind of exciting adventure they'd have next.

The End

Bluebell
Spring fairy

Likes:

blue, blue, blue, and more blue,
turning somersaults in the air, dancing

Dislikes:

finishing second, being told what to do

Daisy
Summer fairy

Likes:

everyone to be friends, bright sunshine,
cheery colors, big fairy hugs

Dislikes:

arguments, cold dark places,
ugly orange dresses

Rosehip
Autumn fairy

Likes:

riding magic ponies, telling Bluebell
what to do, playing the piano, singing

Dislikes:

keeping quiet, boring colors,
not being the center of attention!

Snowdrop
Winter fairy

Likes:

singing fairy songs, cool quiet places, riding her
favorite magical unicorn, making snowfairies

Dislikes:

being too hot, keeping secrets

Don't miss the rest of the series!